JEBEDIAH RUFUS

AN APPALACHIAN TALL TALE

Story and Design By Joshua Gibson

Illustration by Steve McAllister

PUBLISHED BY

Giant Step

DESIGN CO
FRANKLIN COUNTY. VA

Story by Joshua Gibson
Illustration by Steve McAllister
Book design by Joshua Gibson

For more information, please contact
josh@giantstepdesign.com

Jebediah Rufus: An Appalachian Tall Tale
FIRST EDITION

www.giantstepdesign.com

This book is dedicated to...

Christina and our children, Lera, Miles and Silas, who support
everything I do and inspire all sorts of silly ideas

My parents and grandparents, for instilling in me a love of
reading, music, art, family, and tradition

My brothers, for helping shape my sense of humor
and joining me on our own adventures

My New Mexico Philfriends, who helped grow the legend of this story
-J.G.

Sterling and Walter McAllister who taught the value
and wonder of life in Appalachia.
- S.M.

**"The power of imagination
makes us infinite."**
- John Muir

A WORD ABOUT CONTENT...

I am sure to receive notes about this comedic folk tale from those displeased by its subject matter, so here's my disclaimer: you, dear parent, guardian, or teacher, may find that this book is not *entirely appropriate* for young children whom you do not want exposed to (*a*) scary old men who throw bear manure, (*b*) the word "turds," or (*c*) death and very mild violence.

I recommend you read it first then decide for yourselves whether it is appropriate for your children. My own kids were generally ready to handle it by 7 or 8, which was the age at which their mom and I decided that they sufficiently grasped context regarding silly stories, make-believe, and appropriate behavior (*i.e., they knew when and when not to repeat certain words and phrases*). Parents will need to decide for themselves, and I encourage you to preview the subject matter.

But above all else, keep in mind that I wrote this story at around age twelve, so if you are even remotely offended, don't blame me—blame that pimply, innocent adolescent from the 90's.

- J.G.

JEBEDIAH RUFUS

AN APPALACHIAN TALL-TALE

by
Joshua Gibson
&
Steve McAllister

Y'all gather 'round while the fire dies down,
I've got quite a tale to be weavin'
About an old hillbilly who scared me silly
One fateful autumn evenin'.

It was years ago, where the cool winds blow
In the dark Appalachian hills,
Where the bobwhites call & the pines grow tall
Amongst laurels & moonshine stills.

MY STORY IS GHASTLY!

Nerve-rackin' & nasty.
Of an old man, ornery and ruthless—
And my mind can't erase that dreadful chase
Between me and Jebediah Rufus.

See, Ol' Jeb hailed from the town of Crickdale,
He was a hermit most vile and degradin'.
Swore if any man did set foot on his land
A most HEINOUS SURPRISE would be waitin'!

From the fables and lore
All us kids knew the score,
The folk tales grew
Taller and TALLER...
Schoolchildren conferred
And knew not to disturb
Jeb Rufus way deep in the holler

I'd grown up awestruck!
But later as a young buck
I was drawn to
ADVENTURE & GLORY
I was all full of gumption
(And risky assumption)
So decided to test the old stories...

Though some did protest
I set off on my quest,
Said farewell to all whom I knew.
My foolhardy jaunt
To that forbidden old haunt
Was to learn for myself what was true

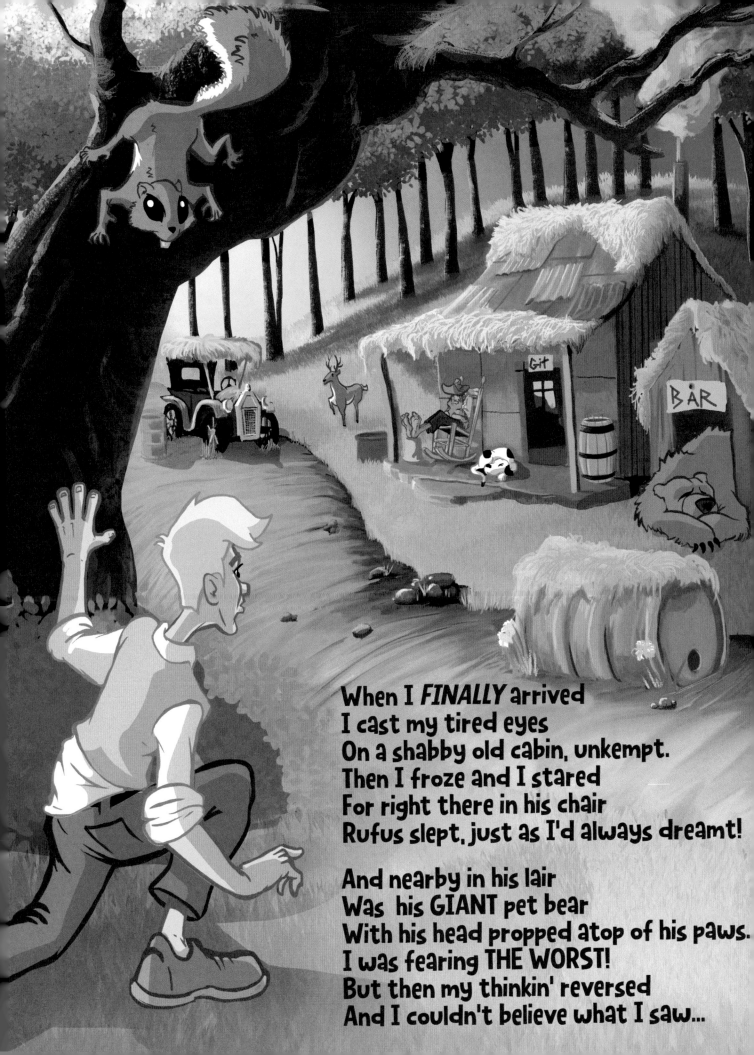

When I *FINALLY* arrived
I cast my tired eyes
On a shabby old cabin, unkempt.
Then I froze and I stared
For right there in his chair
Rufus slept, just as I'd always dreamt!

And nearby in his lair
Was his GIANT pet bear
With his head propped atop of his paws.
I was fearing THE WORST!
But then my thinkin' reversed
And I couldn't believe what I saw...

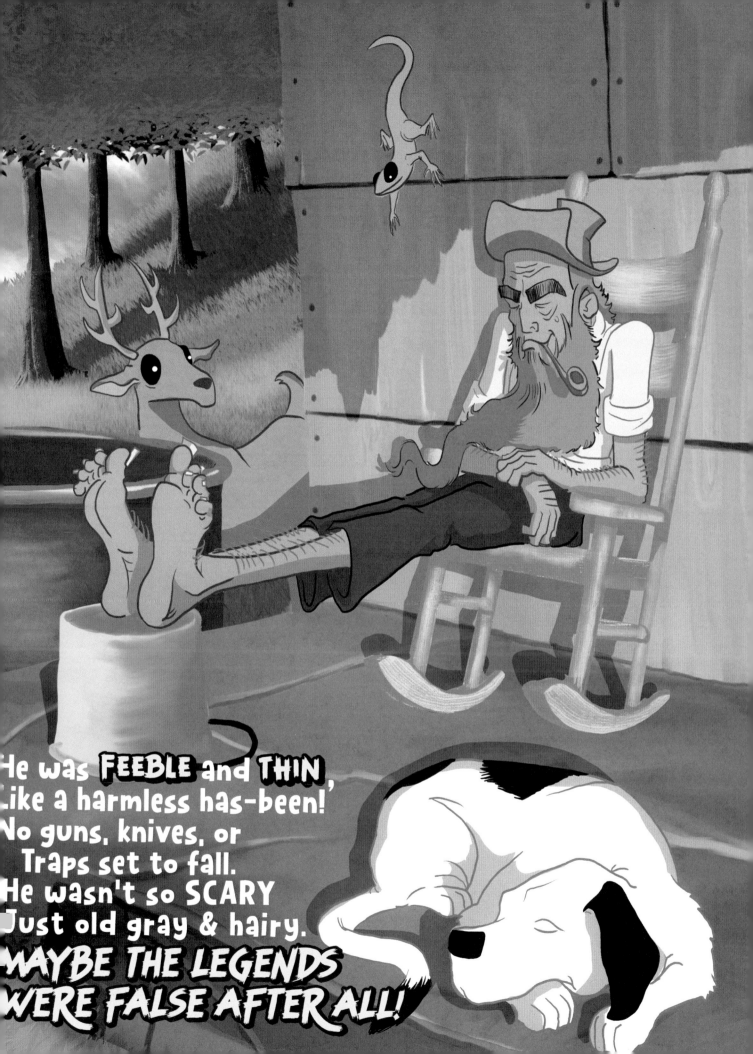

He was **FEEBLE** and **THIN**,
Like a harmless has-been!
No guns, knives, or
    Traps set to fall.
He wasn't so SCARY
Just old gray & hairy.
MAYBE THE LEGENDS
WERE FALSE AFTER ALL!

I'd hiked and I'd rambled
Through rivers and brambles
To look my fears
　　Right in the face.

Well it's go now or quit!
So I mustered my grit
And walked right toward
　　Ol' Jeb's homeplace.

I held out a hand,
Then hollered,

RUFUS, MY MAN!

Just a'grinnin all I was able...

I thought, *I WILL BE HAILED BY ALL OF CRICKDALE*
For debunking the Jeb Rufus fable!

But friends, in that yard
I did let down my guard,
And soon learned that
    My stunt was absurd...

Well OBVIOUSLY
I was bewildered to see
AIRBORNE
BEAR DUNG
A-flyin' my way.

So I stopped and I kneeled
While trying to shield,
And here's what he had to say

"NOW LOOKY HERE, YOU!"

That's my pet bear's poo
A'flying straight for your cranium.
You're lucky as HECK
I ain't wearin' my specs,
Cause then I would REALLY be aimin' em!"

Well being really cautious
Not to get nauseous,
I wiped off the turds and I ran.
I had to hide my hiney,
'Cuz right up behind me
Was Jebediah, with a fully-loaded hand!

I ran like a coward
Toward them woods I'd come outta
And I regretted my ill-conceived plan.
He seemed so darn frail!
But moved like a whitetail,
Hurling smelly bear scat as he ran!

That rickety doofus
Old man Rufus
Chased me all through the woods.
I dodged through the trees
And ran like the breeze
But it just didn't do no good.

He was bombardin' my noggin
But I just kept joggin',
I was bobbin' & weaving & racin'.
Plop after plop
I kept hoping he'd stop,
But Ol' Jeb, he kept right on chasin'!

I ran real hard once I got to my yard,
And I slammed the wood door to my shack.

...But after a while, I didn't hear Jebediah,
So I peeked outside through a crack.

I could see his gray hair
At the bottom of the stairs,
So I knew that he'd fallen down.

I thought,
"AW, WHAT THE HECK!"
And I stepped out
   on the deck
To help him up
   off the ground.

I was sad and surprised to see his closed eyes
And his old bearded mug turned a facin' me.
That cranky ol' cat had a heart attack
Right then, as he was chasin' me.

The world right away felt more boring and gray
Without Jeb out there chasin' off pests.
But it still made me grin that this myth among men
Passed away doin' what he loved best.

And my mind can't erase
The day of the chase
Between me and Jebediah Rufus.

THE END

Critter scat of the Southern Appalachians

GREAT HORNED OWL

Pro - Glows in the dark!
Con - Mouse parts are nasty

RED FOX

Pro - Orange color nice
      for dramatic effect
Con - usually buried in a hole

POSSUM

Pro - Marsupials are pretty nifty,
      I wish I had a natural pouch, too
Con - Their poop has too many ticks

RACCOON

Pro - I like their little mask
Con - They keep stealin'
      all my cornbread

GRAY SQUIRREL

Pro - Acorn chunks help throwin' distance
Con - Squirrels are always actin'
      kinda crazy

EASTERN COTTONTAIL

Pro - Neat little pellets
Con - Smaller than BBs,
      not sticky enough

SNAKE

Pro - Dense, good for slingshot
Con - Snakes are evil!

BOBCAT

Pro - Great velocity in the air
Con - Lots of tiny fish parts

Critter Scat of the Southern Appalachians

WHITETAIL DEER

Pro - Piles of it right here in my garden.
Con - Piles of it all over the garden!

MUSKRAT

Pro - Nice & gooey
Con - Difficult to scavenge from water

COYOTE

Pro - Makes a neat howlin' sound in the air
Con - Mighty wily & hard to catch, need to get me a roadrunner

GROUNDHOG

Pro - Chubby & cute & fun to chase
Con - Can't collect their poop if they beat me to their burrow

SHREW

Pro - Scat is tiny, easy to conceal
Con - Creepy lookin', weird noses

RIVER OTTER

Pro - Mussel shell bits help with impact
Con - Need a sifter to collect from the creek

SKUNK

Pro - Extra smelly on the target
Con - Also extra smelly in my hand!

INDIANA BAT

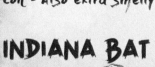

Pro - Sticky, easy to form pellets
Con - I'm scared of caves

BLACK BEAR
(A.K.A. MY PET B'AR, HERCULES)

Pro - Penty of it right here in the bearhouse
Con - Hercules worries I only keep him around for his scat, and that ain't true

A BRIEF HISTORY OF JEBEDIAH RUFUS

Believe it or not, the book you've just read (or had read to you) actually has a pretty long history. No, it's not exactly one of the renowned American tall tales, like *Pecos Bill*, *Johnny Appleseed*, or *John Henry*, but it *was* written 30 years ago, when I was a middle school kid. I created this funny, kind of gross rhyming story around age 12, on a sweltering family car trip to the beach. I took inspiration from my favorite traditional folk legends, tall tales, and stories, while adding my own twists. I set the story in the Appalachians around the time of Prohibition, when moonshine-making was at its height. And of course, when you're an adolescent boy, what's better than adding in old hillbillies, bathroom humor, adventure, and trespassing?

In college, I performed *Jebediah Rufus*—in character—at a nightly campfire program to thousands of visitors to Philmont Scout Ranch in Cimarron, New Mexico. The story was well-received, and I loaned it out to many folks who took it back to their own hometowns to share with others. Once, I even gave permission to a professional storyteller to use it onstage in his next theatrical storytelling competition! Over the course of its life, the story of *Jebediah Rufus* has unexpectedly traveled the world and has entertained a lot of folks.

Once I decided to develop the story into a book, it was important to me that the vibe and artwork of the book honor the Appalachian region and its culture, beauty, and storytelling traditions (despite the weird story content). Illustrator Steve McAllister, a fellow Virginian with his own ties to the Appalachian region, perfected my vision for it, and I am grateful to Steve for lending his amazing talents and for his many improvements to this book.

As one of the most beautiful and ecologically diverse areas on earth, the Appalachians are a special place. I am proud of my family's connection to this region and the strong bonds of family, music, and tradition that hold its communities together. I hope *Jebediah* is enjoyed as a silly escape, and that people appreciate its beginnings as an Appalachian-specific tall tale.

Lastly, a note to parents: I hope you will keep encouraging imagination and make-believe in your children (no matter how weird things can get sometimes). Even as adults, it's best sometimes to not take things so seriously.

— Josh Gibson

ABOUT THE CREATORS

Joshua Gibson is owner and founder of Giant Step Design Co. a design, branding and e-commerce company based in Franklin County, Virginia. He creates artwork and merchandise for Amazon, the music industry, and national brands. He and his wife and children live on a family farm at the foothills of the Blue Ridge Mountains. This is his first children's book.

Steve McAllister is an American illustrator and Virginia native. Steve spent his youth playing in the creeks and hollers of his grandfather's Appalachian farm. He currently resides outside of Richmond, Virginia, with his beautiful wife and children, where he draws, paints, plays his guitar, and creates worlds.

Made in the USA
Middletown, DE
11 November 2021